THE Ring Bear

written by **N.L. Sharp**
illustrated by **Michael T. Hassler Jr.**

ISBN 1-886225-91-5

Dageforde Publishing, Inc.
128 East 13th Street
Crete, Nebraska 68333
www.dageforde.com
1-800-216-8794

Printed in the United States of America

10 9 8 7 6 5 4 3 2 1

For Larry, Scott,
Kevin, and Randy:
Thanks for everything!
N. L. S.

To my mom and dad:
Thanks for all your love
and encouragement.
M. T. H.

Robert loved bears. Real bears and stuffed bears and bears in books. Black bears and brown bears and polar bears. He even loved to eat bears. Graham cracker bears and cinnamon bears and chocolate bears. So he wasn't surprised when his mom said he was going to be the ring bear in his Aunt Jane's wedding.

"What does a ring bear do?" Robert asked.

"You carry the pillow that holds the rings," Mom said.

"What happens if I drop it?" Once, he was carrying his plate to the sink. It dropped and peas rolled all over the kitchen floor.

"Don't worry," Mom said. "The rings will be tied on tight. Even if you drop the pillow, you won't lose the rings."

"What does a ring bear wear?" Robert asked.

"A suit," Mom said. "A black suit with a tail, a white shirt, and a red bow tie."

Robert smiled. I'll look like a panda bear, he thought. This was going to be fun.

Robert wanted to be the best ring bear he could, so he practiced every day. He growled at the dog. He ate berries (which were really grapes) and drank honey (which was really apple juice).

And he crawled around the house with his pillow on his back, trying to keep his glow-in-the-dark ring from falling on the floor.

Finally, there was only one day left before the wedding.

"Robert, it's time for the rehearsal," Mom said.

"Rehearsal? What's that?"

"The rehearsal is like a play. We're going to practice our parts for the wedding so tomorrow we'll know just what to do."

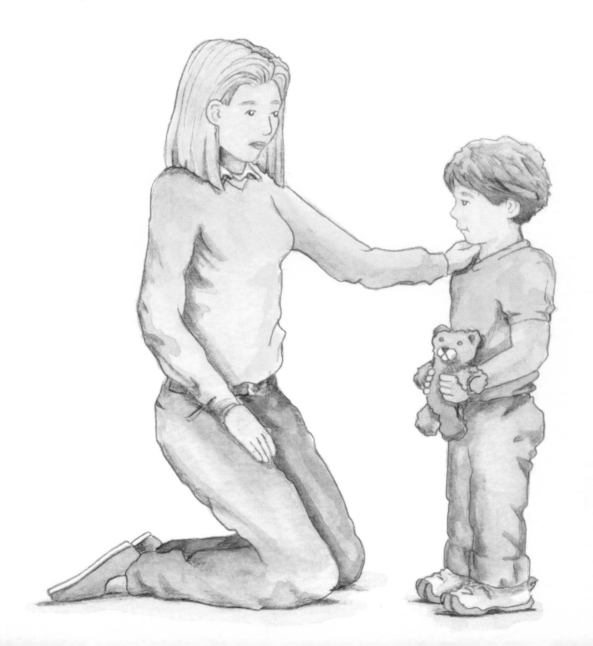

"I've been practicing," Robert said. "Every day."

"Good!" Mom said. "I'm proud of you. But tonight Aunt Jane wants everyone to practice together."

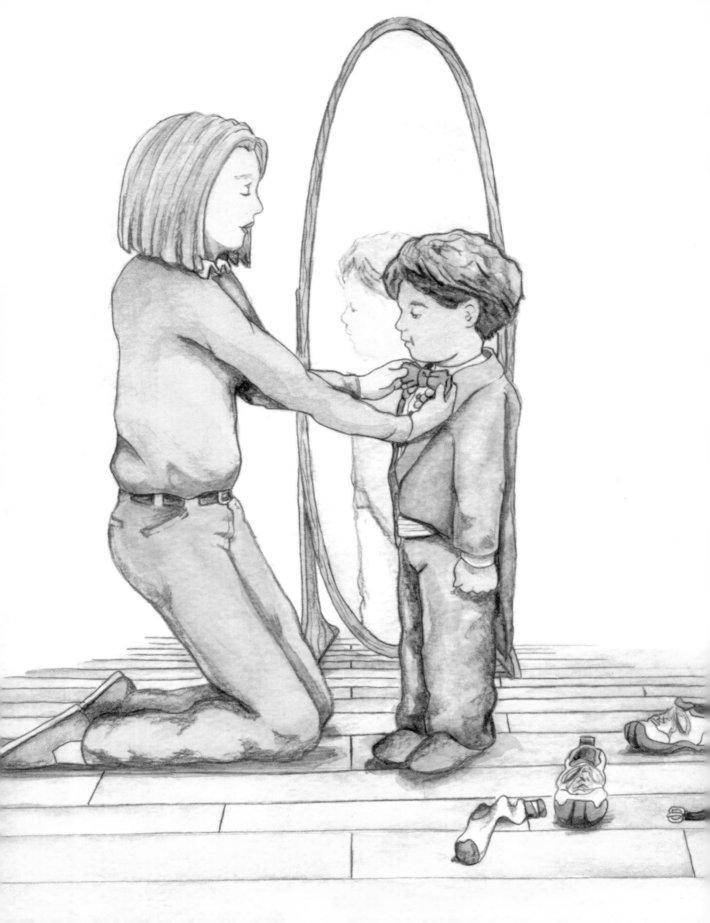

Robert looked at his clothes. "Where's my suit?" he asked.

"Here it is." Mom took a bag out of the closet.

The black suit did not look like a bear suit to Robert. Instead, it looked like something his dad wore when he went to a fancy party.

"Are you sure this is what I'm supposed to wear?" he asked.

"Yes," Mom said.

"Where's the tail?" Robert asked.

"Here." Mom pointed to a long flap on the back of the jacket.

Robert looked at the flap. Then he looked at his bears. Maybe I'm supposed to be a dancing bear, he thought. Like in the circus.

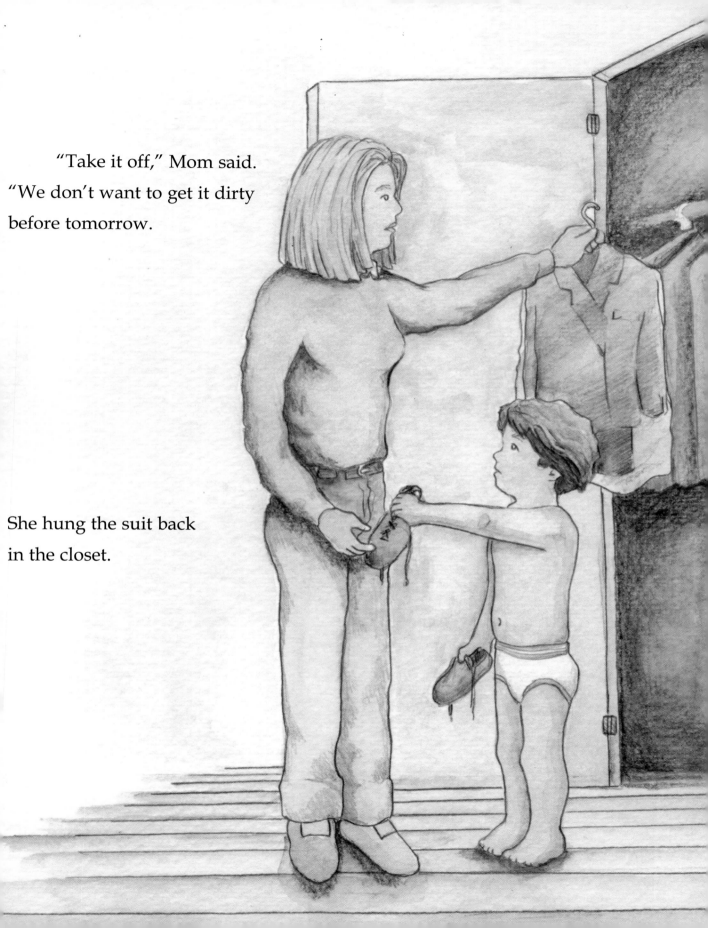

"Take it off," Mom said.
"We don't want to get it dirty
before tomorrow.

She hung the suit back
in the closet.

Soon it was time to go. Robert wondered

where the wedding would be.

Would it be in his grandmother's backyard?

Maybe it was in a park

or at the zoo.

But the car did not go to any of those places.
Instead, his dad drove straight to the church.

"What are we doing here?" Robert asked.
"Is this where the wedding will be?"

"Yes," said Dad. "Didn't you know?"

"No," said Robert. "How can I be a bear when the wedding is in a church?"

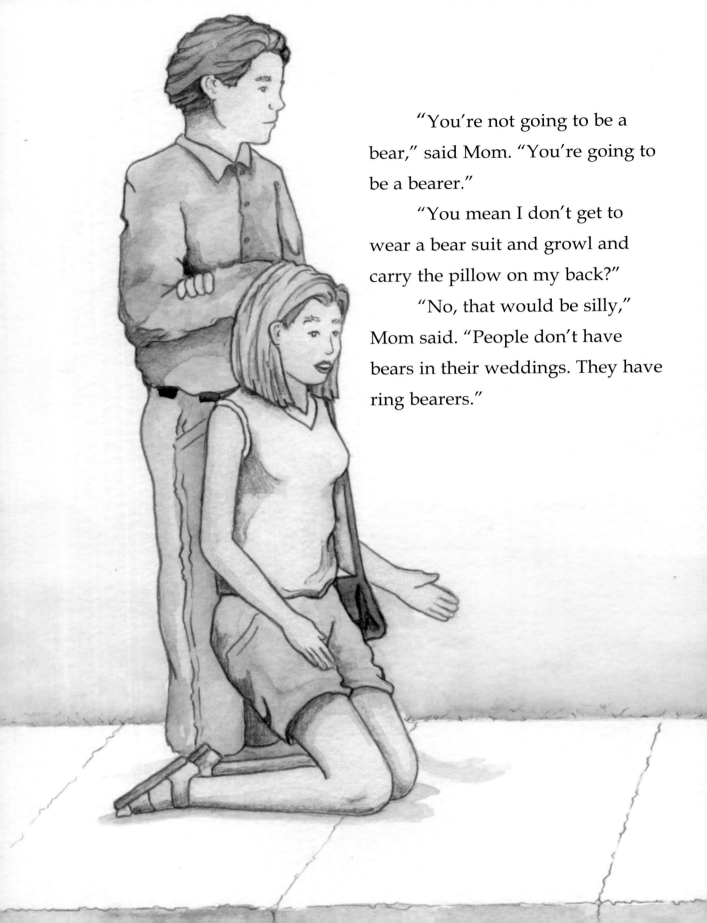

"You're not going to be a bear," said Mom. "You're going to be a bearer."

"You mean I don't get to wear a bear suit and growl and carry the pillow on my back?"

"No, that would be silly," Mom said. "People don't have bears in their weddings. They have ring bearers."

Robert stomped his foot. "I want to be a bear," he said. "If I can't be a bear, I'm not going to be in the wedding!"

"You have to be in the wedding!" Mom insisted. "Aunt Jane needs you. She can't get married without those rings."

"Someone else can carry them," Robert said.

"I don't want someone else," Aunt Jane said. "I want you."

Robert sat down on the curb. He put his hand on his chin.

"Is it true you can't get married without those rings?" he asked.

"Yes, Robert, it is," Aunt Jane said.

"And do you really want me to be the one to carry them?"

"Yes, I do. It wouldn't be the same without you."

Robert growled and took the pillow from Aunt Jane's hand. "I'll do it," he said.

The next day Robert wore his black suit with its long tail, white shirt, and red bow tie. He carried the pillow down the aisle and held the rings until the minister needed them. And everyone agreed, he was the best ring bearer they had ever seen.

Later, at the reception, he growled at the flower girl. He ate berries (which were really mints) and drank honey (which was really punch). And he crawled around on the floor with the pillow on his back, trying to keep the ring pop his new Uncle Dan had given him from falling on the floor. And everyone agreed he was the best ring bear they had ever seen, too.